# Turkey Monster Thanksgiving

# Turkey Monster Thanksgiving

Anne Warren Smith

Albert Whitman & Company
Morton Grove, Illinois

Library of Congress Cataloging-in-Publication Data

Smith, Anne Warren.
Turkey monster Thanksgiving / by Anne Warren Smith.
p. cm.
Summary: When her perfectionist classmate and neighbor plans
an elaborate Thanksgiving dinner, Katie begins to wonder if the
relaxed day she, her father, and her messy little brother usually
enjoy means they are not a "real" family.
ISBN 0-8075-8125-9 (hardcover)
[1. Thanksgiving Day—Fiction. 2. Dinners and dining—Fiction.
3. Single-parent families—Fiction. 4. Family life—Fiction.] I. Title.
PZ7.S6427Tu 2003        [Fic]—dc21        2003004394

The typeface is New Century Schoolbook.
The design is by Susan B. Cohn.

For more information about Albert Whitman & Company,
visit our web site at www.albertwhitman.com.

*For my
grandaughter, Sierra,
&
for Jerry*

# Contents

# 1
# My Socks Don't Match

Dad and Tyler and I like our Thanksgivings easy. Dad says that was always true—even before he and Mom got divorced and she went off to be Roxanne Winter, the famous Country and Western singer. He says that on Thanksgiving we're supposed to wear our pajamas till noon. We eat popcorn, make pizza, and watch the football game on TV.

Dad says our way is a fine way to celebrate a national holiday.

When I found out he might be wrong, it was almost too late—less than two weeks before Thanksgiving. Claire Plummer and I were walking home after school. She had just pointed out that my socks didn't match.

"One is red, and one is orange," I said. "So?"

"Kids like you and me—without mothers at home," Claire said, "have to do things perfectly."

Count on Claire to know what was perfect. Claire had been acting perfect ever since second grade—back when her mother died. I stomped my tennis shoes through a puddle. Of course, *she* was wearing boots.

Claire twirled her sky-blue umbrella and tossed her blond curls—her perfect blond curls. "My father says that when you don't have a mother, people notice socks. They also notice when your hair needs cutting."

"No, they don't," I said. I shook my long bangs out of my eyes.

"And then they say things like 'poor child, she has no mother.'"

"This is a very boring conversation," I said.

"Nobody's going to 'poor child' me. Do you know why?"

I sighed. "Why?"

"My father and I are inviting forty people for Thanksgiving dinner."

I screeched to a halt. I stared at her. "No way!"

"Take a look, smarty." She shrugged out of one strap of her periwinkle blue backpack and unzipped it. Of course, *her* zipper still worked.

She pulled out a roll of paper and held it under her umbrella to keep it out of the rain. As she unrolled it, I saw name after name in Claire's perfect handwriting.

All at once, I envied Claire Plummer, holding that list on that long roll of paper. I could hardly stand it. The only thing Claire and I had in common—besides not having mothers around—was that we both liked to make lists.

"What are *your* plans for Thanksgiving?" she asked.

I couldn't mention pajamas and football and pizza. I decided to lie. I couldn't help it. "We've asked a few people," I said. "Not forty."

"Guess you can't come to our dinner then." Claire pulled out a pencil and drew thick lines through three names on her list. Dad's. Tyler's. Mine.

"Wait a minute," I said.

She looked up. "What's the matter?"

"Nothing," I answered. I watched her tuck everything back into her pack.

"We weren't sure about inviting your little brother anyway," she said. "He's so messy."

"I bet you spilled when you were three, Claire Plummer."

"*I* never needed newspapers all over the table. Are your invitations done?"

"We're on top of things," I said. Another lie. At last, we turned the corner of Benson Street.

"I'm excited. Only thirteen days left till Thanksgiving, Katie." Claire looked both ways and ran across the street to her house.

I ran up on my porch and zigzagged around the wading pool toys, Dad's bike, and Tyler's stroller. I could hear Tyler inside hollering one of his happy songs—the cement mixer song.

I decided to forget about Thanksgiving.

# 2
# Stupid Magazine

Five minutes later, the doorbell rang. "Get it, Katie," Dad called. He was hunched over his computer in the room he'd turned into his office. And, naturally, Tyler was so busy racing his cement mixer across the couch cushions, he never looked up.

It was Claire. She held a magazine out to me like it was something precious. *"Beautiful Living,"* she said, her voice full of respect. "We had an extra."

I put my hands behind my back.

"It tells what to do for Thanksgiving. My father said we really needed it. You, Katie, need it more than we do."

"I don't think so."

She fluttered the pages at me. "It has guest lists, menu lists, grocery lists, decorations lists, to-do lists."

"Lists?" I reached for the magazine. It stunk of perfume. "I don't want this," I said, trying to hand it back. But Claire was staring at the floor. "It really shows," she said.

"What shows?"

"No mother here. This floor is dirty!"

I tossed the magazine at her. "It's been raining. We track stuff in."

Claire pressed the magazine to her chest as if I'd broken the thing. "I brought this for your own good," she said. "So people wouldn't feel sorry."

"Hello, Claire," Dad said. He stood in the hallway with his coffee cup in his hand. "How's your dad?"

"This year, we're doing Thanksgiving the way we used to," Claire said. "My father's already practiced the turkey." She handed the magazine to Dad. "He wanted you and Katie to have this," she said. "He gets good ideas from it."

"Thanks," Dad said. "We could probably use some ideas." He tucked the magazine under his arm.

Claire went partway out the door and then turned back. She waved her umbrella at the toys on the porch steps. "I almost fell," she said.

Dad peered out the door. "You almost fell?"

"A mother would have picked those up," she said.

"Goodbye, Claire." I tugged Dad's sleeve to get him back in and slammed the door. "I wish you didn't make me walk with her," I said.

"It's safer in pairs," Dad said. "I hope you're nice to Claire."

"I'm nice to her. But it's not easy."

Dad looked at Claire's magazine. On the cover, a brown crusty turkey filled a huge silver platter. Dressed-up people stared at it, their mouths all saying, "Ohhhhh."

He handed the magazine to me. "I like pizza for Thanksgiving."

"Me, too," I said.

"You should take this back to Claire," he said.

"Tomorrow." In my room, I tossed the magazine into a pile of papers and turned my radio on to the Country & Western station in case they played one of Mom's songs.

Sometimes they played my favorite, the one about letters from home. That song made Mom think about me. She'd told me so.

Later, I helped Dad fix supper. All our meals were Dad's famous ones, recipes he made up. Tonight it was his famous toasted tuna sandwiches. He lifted the plate of sandwiches over his head and carried it to the table just like a French waiter.

"Wait till you taste these. I put in green chilies," he called.

I could hardly hear over Tyler's new song. "Big engine goes," Tyler roared, "va-room, va-room, va-room." He pounded his fork on his newspapers.

If we ever had forty people for dinner, what would they think about Tyler? "The Plummers," I yelled, "are inviting forty people for Thanksgiving."

Dad sat down and draped a towel across

Tyler's front. "Good for them," he said. "Mr. Plummer is very organized. He also doesn't work for Harold Flagstaff. Mr. Flagstaff has hired me to write a big report, and it's due the night before Thanksgiving."

"Claire said if we don't do Thanksgiving right, people might feel sorry for us."

"Feel sorry?" Dad asked. "Why?"

Tyler squeezed his sandwich and tuna juice dribbled out onto his sleeve. And then he licked it off.

"It's like we're not really a family," I said.

"We have a real family here," Dad said, "even if your mother and I are divorced." He set his sandwich down and leaned toward me. "Harold Flagstaff pays the bills for this real family. As long I write reports for him, we get to eat."

After we finished dinner, Dad scooped Tyler up in his arms. "Time to wash off the dinner," he said. He looked at me. "Join us at the bathtub? Big race tonight. The ducks against the boats."

"Come on, Katie," Tyler said. "We can race Dad."

"Oh, no." Dad shivered in fear. "The two of you against poor me?"

He was right to fear us. Tyler, the ducks, and I beat him and the boats, three times out of four.

# 3
# Twelve Days and Counting

Saturday morning, when Dad brought in the newspaper, he brought in one of Claire's gloves. "She must have dropped it," he said. "Why don't you take it over to her? Take that magazine back, too."

"I can do it Monday," I said, "on the way to school." I was busy right then, drawing a Thanksgiving picture for homework. I had the Pilgrims and Indians playing frisbee and softball. I had Tyler in there, too, but I still needed to draw Dad and me. Plus some kids from fourth grade.

"She could use a visit from a friend."

"Claire doesn't have friends," I said. I drew

a big dish of blueberries in front of Tyler and colored his face blue.

"Ahem," Dad said.

I put down the blue crayon. "Okay, okay."

When Claire opened the door, I smelled chicken soup mixed with fresh paint. I handed over her glove. But I'd forgotten the magazine.

Claire's face was pink with excitement. "Come see our turkey," she said. "My father and I made it for the roof. It's going to glow in the dark up there!"

In their family room, the smell of paint plugged my nose. A huge plywood turkey stood beside the patio doors. Its beady eye glared down at us.

"The pattern in the magazine was little," Claire said. "My father enlarged it."

"It got big, all right." My neck ached from looking up at that mean eye.

"I love getting ready for Thanksgiving," Claire said. She tugged me into the kitchen where good smells bubbled out of a pot on the shining stove.

"Chicken soup?" I asked.

"More than soup," Claire said. "It's one of our dinners for next week." She tapped a list that hung on the refrigerator door. "Monday, Chicken Tomato. Wednesday, Zesty Hummerburgers. Friday, Macaroni Puffaroni. My father makes the exact same things my mother used to make. What are you having?"

"Don't know yet," I said. "Dad decides five minutes before we eat."

Claire frowned as if she didn't believe me. Then she pulled me over to a counter that was stacked with cookbooks and recipes. "Here's what we're planning for Thanksgiving dinner," she said. She held up a paper that had bunches of words on it, some crossed off, some added in. "We have fifteen different things to eat so far," she said. "Of course the turkey is the most important."

"Turkeys aren't so great," I said. "We're having . . ." I stopped. All at once, pizza didn't sound special enough. "I should get back now," I said. "Tyler wants me to play cars."

"You have to play baby stuff with him?" Her nose wrinkled up.

"Goodbye, Claire." I zipped up my coat.

"Just one more thing," Claire said. "We found really nice Thanksgiving invitations." She pulled me into the dining room.

Someone had folded back the yellow tablecloth to make room for orange envelopes and brown and orange cards. *Please Come,* the cards said on the fronts. "I'm doing the insides," Claire said. She opened one and I saw an address and phone number written in her perfect handwriting. "Too bad you won't get one of these," she said.

I looked at the heap of invitations. I almost wished we were still invited. Then I remembered my lie. "We can't," I said. "Company."

"Who are you inviting?"

"Oh," I said, "you wouldn't know them." I pushed past her into the hall.

"Who?" she asked.

I yanked open her front door. "I have to go home now."

"Only twelve days left," she sang.

I ran across the street.

# 4
# "Don't Even THINK About Company!"

**W**hen I got home, I stepped over the toys on our porch and the dirt and leaves on the floor in the hall. But I didn't see the Legos. I slipped and fell down. My elbow whammed the closet door. "Dad!" I yelled.

"In the kitchen," he called back.

I walked a narrow path between toys and newspapers and jackets and shoes. In our kitchen, the stove did not shine. Grocery bags, cans of spices, and cereal boxes spilled across the counters. The sink held three banana peels, Tyler's toast edges, and five old coffee filters.

"I slipped on some Legos," I said. "My elbow's broken."

"Rub it," Dad said. "It'll feel better." He poured hot water from the kettle, making another cup of coffee. "Tyler's dump truck had a serious accident. We should close the highway."

"Claire is right," I said. I couldn't believe I was saying such a thing out loud.

Dad wasn't listening. He stirred the coffee grounds with the tip of a knife and added more water. He sniffed at his mug and smiled. "Ahh," he said.

"Claire's house looks nice," I said. "Like a real family lives there. You can walk around without falling on things."

"No three-year-old at that house." Dad sipped and swallowed. "Makes a difference." He sighed. "We'll pick things up later. Right now, I've got this deadline. This report."

"It's okay, Dad. Except . . ."

He raised his eyebrows.

"They've got food cooking. And invitations. And decorations." I picked up a banana peel and tossed it into the trash.

He set his mug on the counter and stared

into it. "Maybe they want everything to be the way it was before Claire's mother died," he said. "Before the accident."

"Because they miss her?"

He nodded.

I thought about that. "We miss Mom, too," I said. "She's been gone three years. But at least, she's alive. We still get to see her . . ."

"Your mom is doing something hard, trying to be a professional singer." Dad put his arm around me. "But she loves it. You know that she loves you and Tyler, too."

"I wish we could see her more." I blinked at something in my eye.

He cleared his throat. "Christmas. You'll be with her then. At your grandma's."

I pushed my nose into Dad's flannel shirt and smelled coffee and books and sadness about Mom. "If she was here," I said, "we'd do Thanksgiving better."

"Maybe." He tipped my head up so I was looking at him. "Aren't we doing okay without her?"

"Most of the time, we do fine," I told him.

"But we should plan something special."

"Katie . . ."

"At least we should dress up," I said. "Mom gave me a dress last Christmas."

Dad nodded. "I remember it."

"I think it's in my closet," I said.

He smoothed my bangs out of my eyes. "Wear your dress. But I really like wearing pajamas on Thanksgiving."

I shook my bangs back down. "The Pilgrims didn't wear pajamas. They dressed up and cooked special food. They had company."

"You forget Flagstaff's report," he said. "It's due Wednesday night. I'll be working on it all week. If we have to celebrate, we can't do it on Thursday. We'll do it the next Saturday. Or Sunday."

"Thanksgiving dinner has to be on Thanksgiving Day." I grabbed another banana peel and threw it in the trash. "I like planning things. I planned your birthday last summer."

"You're a great planner." He patted the top of my head and grinned. "All right," he said. "Plan dinner for us. Plan decorations. But no company. Don't even THINK about company."

As he went down the hall to his office, I pushed breakfast dishes to the other end of the big table. I found a pencil and a pad of yellow paper.

"DECORATIONS," I wrote. I'd draw things. That would be easy! I'd get out my big roll of paper and draw Pilgrims and Indians and turkeys. Put them up in every room. I wrote "Pilgrims. Indians. Turkeys."

New piece of paper.

"WHAT TO WEAR." I tapped my pencil. "Me—my dress. Find it." I stared down the hall toward Dad's office. Would he change his mind? No, he wouldn't. I wrote, "Dad—best pajamas. NOT purple smiley-face ones. Tyler—train jammies." He loved his train jammies. He had four sets of them.

Next list.

"FOOD. Popcorn. Pizza (Dad's famous)." I pictured it. Extra melty cheese for me. Heaps of onions and garlic for Dad. Whole black olives for Tyler to wear on his fingers. Yum!

I couldn't decide on the best dessert.

Strawberry ice cream sandwiches? Lemon yogurt popsicles? I wrote them both down. On such a special day, we would have two desserts.

Before I reached for the next sheet of paper, I thought a long time. My decorations were terrific. My food was wonderful. If only we could have company!

I made sure Dad was in his office where he couldn't see me, and then I wrote two words in big, dark letters:

**GUEST LIST**

# 5
# Monster!

**B**y Sunday morning, I had a bunch of lists.

GUEST LIST

DECORATIONS LIST

FOOD LIST

GROCERY LIST

WHAT TO WEAR LIST

They looked great! I tacked each one, except for the guest list, onto my bulletin board. The guest list I hid in my sock drawer.

So far, that list had only nine people. Mr. and Mrs. Anderson from next door, plus Nancy, the lady who brings the mail, plus Sierra, my best friend, and her mom and dad. Plus Dad and Tyler and me. Nine! I needed lots more.

Sunday afternoon, Claire and Mr. Plummer gave up on putting their turkey on the roof. It was too big. Instead, they set it on the lawn where it glared at everyone who walked by.

Tyler peeked out the front window. "We should have one of those," he said.

"You wouldn't want it if you could see it up close," I teased him. "It's a mean turkey."

"Mean turkey? A monster turkey?"

"There's no such thing," I said.

Dad came to look. "I don't know how Claire's dad finds time to do so many projects."

Tyler tugged at the drapes. "It IS a monster," he said. "That turkey monster's looking in here!"

I pulled the drapes closed and made it dark in the living room. We turned some blankets into caves and pretended bats were flying out of the ceiling light. Then, we switched from bats to turkey monsters. Tyler kept peeking through the drapes.

"Help, help," he yelled. "Turkey monster's opening his mouth!"

I made my voice low and scary. "Turkey

monsters come to life on Thanksgiving Day. They eat kids."

"Run, kids," Tyler shrieked. Then we raced across the room and leaped into our blanket caves. We did that over and over until finally Dad finished his office work and made us put away the blankets.

Later, while Dad washed Tyler's dinner off in the bath, I found Claire's magazine. According to *Beautiful Living*, everyone in the United States, mother or no mother, would be celebrating Thanksgiving the way the Plummers were doing it. Every kitchen would be cooking lots of food. Every house would be decorated inside and out.

I flopped down on my bed with my decorations list. Where I'd written TURKEY ON THE ROOF, I crossed out ROOF. My turkey would go on the front door. Best of all, *my* turkey would be a happy one.

While I cut and colored, I kept trying to think of more people for my guest list. I imagined bunches of them sitting at our pretty table getting ready to eat fifteen kinds of food.

But if there were going to be guests, I'd need invitations. Baby turkeys would make perfect invitations. I got more paper out and pretty soon a big flock of baby turkeys lay all over my bed. On Thanksgiving Day, people would line up on my sidewalk. They'd stretch around the block like at the movies, all of them waiting to come to my wonderful dinner.

I didn't hear Dad put Tyler to bed. I didn't hear him come up behind me until he was right there. "Those look like invitations," he said.

Snip! Off went a baby turkey's head!

"I told you, Katie," Dad said. "No company!"

All at once, words I hadn't planned to say came out of my mouth. "These are for practice, Dad. For next year."

"Ah," he said. I could tell he didn't believe me.

I reached for the big turkey. "This one's for the front door. What do you think?"

"Not evil enough," he said.

"Dad!"

"No, really. I like the smile."

"I made a grocery list."

He raised his eyebrows.

"Next time we go to the store, let's get some stuff to go with our pizza. I can cook some special dishes ahead of time. That's what Mr. Plummer is doing."

"Hm," he said. "Don't you have any homework?"

"I had to draw a picture. That was all the sub gave us. Ms. Morgan's been sick. I hope she comes back tomorrow."

Dad turned the big turkey upside down and balanced it on its head. Then he made it peck at scraps of paper on my bed. "You like Ms. Morgan pretty well?"

"The whole fourth grade likes her. She's wonderful. Oh, I wish *she* . . ."

Dad looked at me.

"I mean," I said, "*next* year, maybe we can invite Ms. Morgan to Thanksgiving dinner."

"But not *this* year," Dad said.

"Okay, okay." I gathered up the little turkeys. "These were a waste of time."

"They're cute," Dad said. "Use them for decorations."

I sighed. "I'll stick them on the windows. They can look out."

"Good idea." Dad reached for the newspaper and went to lie on the couch.

Look out at nothing, I thought. Only an empty sidewalk, empty front yard, empty driveway.

No long lines of happy people. No one at all coming to my dinner.

# 6
# Room Father Strikes

On Monday morning, Ms. Morgan was back.

I was so glad to see her, I couldn't help myself. I imagined her sitting at my Thanksgiving table. I heard her gasp as she admired all my decorations. "May I take a picture?" Ms. Morgan would ask.

But I couldn't ask Ms. Morgan to Thanksgiving dinner. I couldn't ask anyone at all.

"Take out nice paper," Ms. Morgan was saying. "We need to write thank-you notes to the baker we visited before I got sick." On the board, she wrote a list of words we might need. Then, she wrote a sample note with the date and "Dear Mr. McKenzie," at the top and

"Sincerely yours," at the bottom. "Write the middle part in your own words," she said.

I wrote:

> Dear Mr. McKenzie,
>
> Thank you for giving us rolls to eat. I think you are lucky to work in a bakery. I'm sorry you have to get up when it is still dark.
>
> Sincerely yours,
> Katie Jordan

Everyone else was still writing. I pulled out another piece of paper. Just for practice, I wrote:

> Dear Ms. Morgan,
>
> Please come to our Thanksgiving dinner.
>
> Sincerely yours,
> Katie Jordan

As soon as Ms. Morgan started to pick up our thank-you notes, I stuffed the practice Thanksgiving invitation into my pocket.

Ms. Morgan looked at each note as she picked it up. "Very nice," she said. "Very nice."

When she got to me, she looked surprised. "Especially nice," she said. And then, she winked.

Why was she winking?

She picked up all the other notes. Had I spelled "bakery" wrong? I checked the board. No, I'd spelled it right.

Someone knocked at the classroom door.

Mr. Plummer stood there, holding a tray of cupcakes.

"Room father at your service," he said.

"This is a surprise," Ms. Morgan said.

"I brought these to celebrate your return. Chocolate cupcakes."

Everyone cheered.

Claire's dad placed the tray on Ms. Morgan's desk. Then, he winked at Claire and slipped an orange envelope under the tray. Fourth grade was full of winks this morning.

Mr. Plummer glanced at his watch. "Got to get back to work," he said. He waved at the whole class, almost like Santa Claus, but without the ho, ho, ho. As he went out the door, I stopped smiling about the cupcakes.

I'd seen that orange envelope before. Mr. Plummer had just invited Ms. Morgan to Thanksgiving dinner. Now, even if Dad changed his mind about company, she would go to Claire's house. Not mine.

# 7
# Things Get Worse

In the school bathroom before recess, I took out the practice invitation. I couldn't even bring myself to read it. I ripped it up and threw the tiny pieces into the toilet. I flushed three times.

My lists were at home. I couldn't wait to flush them, too. If I couldn't have Ms. Morgan for Thanksgiving dinner, I didn't want to do anything.

Claire went to ballet on Mondays after school, so Dad pushed Tyler in the stroller to pick me up. Since it was raining, we crowded under Dad's big striped umbrella. As soon as we turned the corner of our block, Tyler started to howl. "Don't let him peck me." He shook a stick at Claire's turkey.

"That was just a game," I told him.

"He eats little kids," Tyler whined. "Keep him away from me."

We parked Tyler's stroller on the front porch. As soon as I got inside, I ran to get the *Beautiful Living* magazine, the door turkey, and the flock of little turkeys. I threw everything into the trash. "You don't have to worry about Thanksgiving dinner," I told Dad.

"How come?"

"It's too much trouble. I'm not going to do it."

"Great!" Dad said.

That night, Dad made his famous stir fry. First he fried up onions and garlic. Then he threw in whatever veggies were getting bendy in the refrigerator. On stir-fry nights, Tyler ate peanut butter sandwiches. First, he stuck them full of holes with his chopsticks. Dad passed me the soy sauce and smiled at the face I was making. "He's going through a playing-with-his-food stage," he said.

"He's sickening," I said. All at once, I was mad about no Thanksgiving. Mad at Tyler.

Mad at Dad. Mad at Mom for going off and leaving us. I pushed back my chair and stood up. "We're a stupid family!" I yelled.

Dad stood up, too. "That's not true."

"It's a good thing we're not having Thanksgiving dinner," I shouted. "How can anyone eat next to . . . that!" I pointed at Tyler. "He has peanut butter up his nose. I'm going to throw up!"

Tyler looked at me, surprised. He stuck his finger up his nose, checking for peanut butter.

"We'll talk about this later." Dad sat back down.

"Mom would make sure he ate right. And she'd make dinner, and we'd have company." I scraped my plate into the garbage.

"Your mother hated to cook," Dad said. He tapped his plate with his chopsticks. "By the way, she called this morning."

I stared at him. "You talked to her?"

He nodded. "She'll call you and Tyler this weekend. She called me because she just got a really good manager. He's booked her in Branson, Missouri. It's her big break."

"Will she be able to do Christmas?"

"She'll be able to do Christmas." Dad wiped Tyler's face with a paper napkin.

I went to my bedroom to hug my pillow and listen to Mom's CD. Hearing her sing only made me realize how far away she was. How busy she was with her new life—a life without me, and Dad, and Tyler. Dad said she hated to cook. I didn't remember that.

But I knew one thing. If Mom was here, she'd want company. I remembered her parties. They were always music jam sessions. Instrument cases stacked in the living room. People singing backup, telling her how good she was, how she ought to go to Nashville.

"Soon as I get my figure back, I'll try it," she'd said. She'd patted her tummy where it still stuck out from having Tyler.

And Dad? Where was he? Then I remembered him jiggling up and down, burping Tyler in time to the music. His face looking as if he already knew she'd never come back.

# 8
# A Delicious Secret

Tuesday morning, Claire wore blue sunglasses. Pretty dumb since it was pouring down rain. "I have to wear these," she said. "I look terrible. I cried all night."

"How come?" I asked.

"Ms. Morgan called us last night. She can't come to our house on Thanksgiving. She got another invitation first." She lifted the sunglasses, and I could see her eyes were a little bit pink. She dropped the blue sunglasses back onto her nose. "I'm going to wear these all day," she said with a sigh. "It's okay. They match my tights."

At school, every time I looked at Ms. Morgan I thought about how she was going to be at somebody else's house for Thanksgiving dinner. It was almost time to go home when she called me up to her desk. "Thank you very much," she said.

I stared at the top of her desk in confusion. What was she thanking me for?

Her silver bracelets clinked together as she smoothed a piece of paper. "You wrote a very nice invitation," she said.

I stared at the note I wrote yesterday. I'd stuffed the wrong paper into my pocket. I'd turned in the invitation instead of the thank-you note! No wonder she'd winked at me.

"Anyway," she continued, "I wanted to be sure your dad knows you invited me?" Her voice was a question.

My mind flew in a hundred directions. Ms. Morgan got my invitation first? Well, yes, she did. "Oh, yes," I heard myself say. "We were talking about it just last night."

"I'm so glad," Ms. Morgan said. "Will there be many of us? A big group?"

"I don't know yet," I said. "For sure, you and Dad and me and Tyler." Disgusting, gross

Tyler. We would have to fix his manners. We definitely wouldn't serve peanut butter.

She glanced up at the clock. "Time to put things away, class," she announced. She squeezed my hand and then bent close to me. Her dark hair smelled like vanilla pudding. "We need to keep this a secret," she said. "Sometimes the other children think it's not fair if the teacher goes to one child's house."

She squeezed my hand again, and I raced back to my desk. Soon as I got home, I had to get my lists out of the trash.

After supper, I curled up with *Beautiful Living* magazine. Every page had great ideas. "She's coming," I whispered. I added strings of cranberries and popcorn to my decorations list.

As I turned the pages, I heard commercials on my radio. "You'll want the very best for your Thanksgiving company," the announcer kept saying. "For Ms. Morgan," I whispered. I looked one more time at the magazine cover. For Ms. Morgan, I thought, maybe we should have turkey.

The radio also said I needed mums from

Francie's Florist. Extra chairs from Party Rents. Mrs. Shaftoe's frozen pies. Birdover's cranberry candies. Plampton's coffee.

I wrote down everything. Just in case.

Ms. Morgan was going to love Thanksgiving at our house.

# 9
# Claire Takes Pictures

Wednesday morning, I told Dad I wanted to make decorations after all. I gave him a list of what I needed.

"Fine," he said. "The house will look very nice."

That day our class had a field trip to the Fire Department. The fire chief let us hold the big hose while water whooshed out at a pretend fire. She pushed a button in the truck and turned on the siren. We all covered our ears. The best part was after that when we got to practice escaping from a little house the Fire Department had built there.

"My mom burned the carrots last night," Sierra told the fire chief. "We didn't have to eat them."

"We don't burn food at our house," Claire said.

Sierra and I moved away from Claire to stand on the other side of the circle. "Are you on Claire's guest list for Thanksgiving?" Sierra whispered.

I shook my head. "Not any more. How about you?"

"We're going to Grandpa Jack's," Sierra whispered.

Ms. Morgan shook her finger at us. We hushed. But now I knew Sierra and her parents couldn't come to my house.

After school, I let Tyler wear the Fire Department badge one of the firefighters had pinned to my jacket. I gave Dad our handouts about smoke alarms and fire extinguishers.

"We'll get new batteries for the smoke alarm next time we go to the store," Dad said. "And a fire extinguisher, too. I hope we never have a fire, but if we do, we'll be prepared."

"Did you get the cranberries for me?" I asked. "And the popcorn?"

"Sure did," he answered.

"I'll make them into those strings," I told him. "The kind you hang up?"

"Festoons?" he asked.

"I'm going to put festoons over every window and every door. First, I have to pop the popcorn. Then I have to find a needle and thread."

"If there's popcorn," Dad said, "Thanksgiving can't be all bad."

"What do turkeys eat?" Tyler asked Dad.

"They love corn," Dad told him. "Corn, the way it is before it's popped."

All at once I knew how to fix Tyler. "They eat little kids who spill at the table," I whispered as soon as Dad went back to his office.

"No, Katie!" Tyler hollered.

"Especially if there's company," I said.

"Don't let him get me," Tyler said. He made me pull the drapes in the living room and lock the front door. He worried about that turkey monster right up until bedtime.

Thursday morning before school, Claire stood under her blue umbrella, gazing at her house. "Isn't our porch beautiful?" she asked.

I had to say yes. Enormous pumpkins marched up the corners of the steps. Little pumpkins and gourds snuggled between them. Cornstalk trees stood on either side of the front door, tied with floppy orange bows. More orange bows perched at the corners of the door and windows. A wreath of greens and straw and tiny gourds filled the center of the door.

"We're going to make a stuffed Pilgrim lady to sit in the porch swing." Claire twirled her umbrella. Raindrops sprayed off it into my face.

I stepped back, out of the way.

"I took pictures of my front porch," Claire said. "I also took one of your porch."

I turned to look. All at once, Tyler's stroller, the wading pool, the water toys, and Dad's old bicycle really showed. "It'll be just as nice as yours," I said. "We're going to use festoons."

"Only seven more days," Claire said.

That afternoon after school, I listened for Mom's songs on the radio while I strung popcorn and cranberries. The Thanksgiving commercials were louder today. "Don't be caught short for the holidays," someone shouted. "Check your candle supply." The next ad was for something to ease that stomachache that "is sure to follow your bountiful Thanksgiving dinner."

Bountiful? I had to get Dad used to the turkey idea. I also had to get started on the other food.

I found my grocery list and  went into Dad's office. "Are we by any chance out of something?" I asked.

"Bread," he answered.

At the store, we filled our cart with cans of sweet potatoes, green beans, and fruit. Tyler sat in the middle of the cart, singing a quiet song to the cans. "Don't you cry. Don't you cry," he sang. "We'll open you up so you can play."

All the ladies in the store thought he was cute.

"Are you sure you can make these dishes without my help?" Dad asked me.

"I'm pretty sure," I said. "The magazine said these were for the time-stressed woman. This week I'll keep making decorations. And then, I'll make Sweet Potato Brulée, Green Beans Deluxe, and a Cranberry Tower."

"She is very organized," Dad said to the woman behind us in the checkout line.

It was time to tell him. "And you'll do the turkey," I said.

Dad's grin went away. "We're not doing a turkey."

"Everybody's doing a turkey," I said. "Look!" I waved my hand at the magazines in the rack next to us. Every magazine had a turkey on the cover!

"You can do it," said the woman.

I patted Dad's arm. "You have me to help you," I said.

# 10
# More Company Needed

The next morning, Claire started again about Thanksgiving. "I'm going to dress up like a Pilgrim," she said. "My dress will be blue, of course."

"We have to hurry," I said, speeding up. I'd completely forgotten to look for my dress. I couldn't think up a good centerpiece for the table. The festoons were taking forever. And I had to invite more people. But then I'd be in bigger trouble with Dad.

"Is everybody on your list coming?" I asked.

"Twenty people said yes," she said. "My father says that's a perfect number."

I had one. One guest was not okay. Worries prickled at me all day at school. Finally, the bell rang to dismiss us.

Since it was Friday, with no ballet or piano lessons, Claire and I had to walk home from school together. "Tomorrow, you'll be able to see our stuffed Pilgrim lady," Claire said as she started across the street to her house. "Her hair is blond and curly, just like mine."

"Too bad," I said.

"That's not either too bad, Ms. Smarty." Claire stabbed her umbrella into the curb. "Most of tomorrow, I'll be taking pictures."

"You better not take any more of my house," I said. I ran down the block to meet Nancy, the mail delivery lady.

She peeled our mail off her bundle and handed it to me. "Hope I brought you some riches," she said. She always said that.

Could I ask Nancy to my dinner? I couldn't decide. "What do you do for Thanksgiving?" I asked.

"Cook for all my in-laws," she said. "And they want their turkey a particular shade of brown."

My guest list had just gotten shorter.

I carried the mail inside and got ready to

string some more cranberries.

Saturday morning, Claire phoned. "Take a look," she said.

"I'm too busy," I said. I hung up.

I ran to the living room to peek through the drapes.

"Is it alive now?" Tyler asked, tearing himself away from *Sesame Street* and sticking his thumb into his mouth, something he hadn't done in ages.

"Not yet," I said. "But now they've got a stuffed lady. She's sitting in their porch swing."

Tyler climbed up beside me to look. "Wow," he said. "She is so beeyootiful."

"I don't think so," I said.

"There's Claire," he said. "What's she doing?"

"Taking a picture," I answered. "Of our house." Something had to be done about our front porch.

Later, while Tyler napped and Dad worked on his report, I pulled the wading pool off the porch and stashed it under the house. I found a place out of the rain for Dad's old bike and all the toys. The fence between our house and the Anderson's was covered with green leaves—some kind of vine. Instant festoons!

I cut off long pieces with scissors. After that, all I needed were thumbtacks and my box of old shoestrings. With green vines draped over the railing and around the door, my porch looked wonderful. Claire Plummer could snap all the pictures she wanted.

Next door, the Andersons were stepping out for their daily walk. Surely, Dad wouldn't mind if the Andersons came to Thanksgiving dinner.

But before I could ask them, Claire and her dad brought out more pumpkins for the steps.

"Your porch is the talk of the neighborhood," Mrs. Anderson hollered across the street to Mr. Plummer.

"We're having fun over here," Mr. Plummer called back. "Got lots more ideas, too."

"We're looking forward to Thanksgiving dinner with you," Mrs. Anderson yodeled.

It took a minute before I realized what I'd

just heard. The Andersons were going to the Plummers. Nancy would be cooking for her in-laws. Sierra would be with her Grandpa Jack.

Ms. Morgan was my only guest.

# 11
# Caught!

Claire said Thanksgiving dinner was supposed to start with appetizers. On Sunday morning, I leafed through the pages of the magazine till I found a picture of a cracker with a dab of cream cheese and tiny green leaves on top. "What is p-a-r-s-l-e-y?" I asked Dad. "Do I hate it?"

"Parsley," he answered. He tipped his glasses up on his forehead and put his finger on the computer screen so he wouldn't lose his place. "It's sort of like grass. Nobody hates it."

"Should I use grass?" I asked. "Or can we buy this stuff?"

"Parsley is at the store. Next to the spinach."

"Great!" I told him. "We'll have this at the beginning of Thanksgiving dinner. As soon as . . ." I stopped, just in time.

"As soon as what?" he asked.

"As soon as I put them on a pretty plate," I said. "I'll make them Thursday morning, while the turkey cooks."

He slumped over his keyboard. "I can't think about that turkey."

I waved the magazine at him. "Don't worry, Dad. All the turkey answers are right here."

The phone rang and Dad picked it up. It was Mom, calling from Nashville. First, she talked to Dad. Then to Tyler. Finally, it was my turn. "What are you up to?" she asked. I loved hearing her voice. Even Mom's talking sounded like singing.

"I'm getting us ready for Thanksgiving," I told her. I described the festoons and the turkey on the door. "I wish you could come to our dinner."

"I wish I could, too. You know what? I might be working Thanksgiving Day. It's pretty frantic here." She covered the phone and talked to someone. "Look, honey," she said when she came back, "I'm afraid I've got to go. I'll call next Saturday and talk to you first. I want to hear all about your dinner."

After we hung up, I went to my bedroom and stared at the poster I'd hung next to my dresser. Mom sure didn't look like a mom in her white cowboy boots and tight jeans and a sparkled red top. "I'm going to wear the dress you gave me," I told the poster.

It took a while to find it in my closet. It was blue! I'd forgotten that. The blue ruffled collar and blue skinny sleeves reminded me of Claire Plummer. I shrugged out of my tee shirt and jeans and pulled the dress over my head. Stuck!

"Ahem," said Dad's voice. "Is that dress holding you prisoner?"

"It's too small." I pulled it off and threw it on the floor. "Anyway, I don't like it."

Dad nodded. "It's a nice dress, but it doesn't look like you. Your mother . . ." He stopped.

I pulled on my jeans and shirt. "She doesn't even know what I like."

He stood there a moment without speaking. Then he wiggled his shoulders and rubbed his back against the door frame like a bear rubbing against a tree. "I need a break from Flagstaff's report. Shall we take Tyler to the park? It's not raining."

I kicked the blue dress under my bed. I didn't feel like going anywhere. But then, I changed my mind. "Let's go."

After dinner that night, Dad put me on bathtub duty. My job was to sit on the toilet seat with my book and make sure Tyler didn't go underwater or flood the bathroom.

Dad was back at his desk across the hall from us. I could hear his fingers racing across the computer keys. That report was sure keeping him busy. His phone rang. "Hello," he said.

Tyler splashed in the tub. "Chug-a, chug-a." He whammed two tugboats together.

"Don't get my book wet," I told him.

Dad's voice suddenly got louder. "Ms. Morgan?" he asked. And then he closed his office door, and I couldn't hear him at all.

# 12
# Dad Makes a List

**A** few minutes later, Dad came into the bathroom. He took his glasses off as they clouded over with steam. "That was your teacher."

"Oh?" I closed my book and pressed it against my aching stomach.

"She thinks we're having company for Thanksgiving dinner."

I swallowed. My ears crackled.

"She thinks SHE is our company for Thanksgiving dinner."

I sagged over. My book stuck sharp corners into my chest.

"She called to say she's bringing two pies." Dad's voice was tired. He rubbed his forehead. "Who else is coming?"

"Just her. No one else."

"Didn't you hear me say 'no company'?" he asked.

Tyler stared at Dad with big, round eyes. "Get me out now." He stood up and tub water sloshed around his knees. "I want my train jammies."

Dad reached for the towel and lifted Tyler out of the tub.

The tub water gurgled down the drain.

"I wanted to watch the game and enjoy my family," he said in that same tired voice. "I wanted to get this report done. And then, I wanted to relax."

"Can I have a story?" Tyler asked. His chin wobbled. His eyes filled with tears.

"Of course," Dad said. He carried Tyler out of the bathroom.

While Dad read to Tyler, I huddled on my bed. Hiccups filled up my chest. Hiccupped out of my mouth.

Once Tyler was in bed, Dad came into my room. "How did this happen?" he asked. "This Thanksgiving thing has turned into a monster."

I hugged my pillow against my sore chest

and told him about the extra invitation and how it got delivered. "I'm sorry, Dad."

"Nothing is ready," he said.

"We have most of the groceries," I told him. "Tomorrow I'll make the Sweet Potato Brulée. Tuesday, the Green Beans Deluxe. Wednesday, the Cranberry Tower. It's under control, Dad."

Dad stared at my lists on the bulletin board. "It's different now that there's company." He found a piece of paper and a pencil and started making a list of his own. "Glasses that match. Cream for coffee."

"We'll clean house Thursday morning," I told him. "While the turkey is cooking."

He groaned. But he wrote "TURKEY!" on his list.

"Ms. Morgan's bringing the dessert." I crossed off popsicles and ice cream sandwiches.

"Real butter," he said, writing furiously. "We used to have real napkins. Where'd they go?"

"They turned into diapers for Tyler's bear. Maybe we can find them?"

"We'll buy paper."

"We need a table centerpiece, Dad."

"Where's that turkey poster you made?"

"On the front door."

"It's now for the table," Dad said. He reached over and crossed CENTERPIECE??? off my list.

His list got very long. He frowned at it for a while. "Too much to do," he said finally.

"I didn't know you liked making lists," I said.

"It's not a matter of liking," he said. "It's a matter of necessity."

"I'm worried about one thing," I told him. "Tyler at the table."

"He's just a little boy."

"He's awful," I said.

"We'll work on it." Dad rested his forehead on his hand.

"Are you still mad?" I could feel my hiccups waiting to start again.

"I'm not mad," he said. "I'm worried we can't get everything done in time."

# 13
# The First Vegetable

Tell me your menu," Claire said as we started to school on Monday morning.

I told her.

"You have to have lots more than that! Someone might be allergic!"

"What?"

"Most people are allergic," she said. "You have to serve lots of food, so if they're allergic to one thing, they can pick something else. Your company doesn't want to get a rash."

I pictured Ms. Morgan looking wistfully at all the food. "No thank you," she'd say. "I'm allergic. Maybe I could eat a sandwich instead." Dad would get out the peanut butter. Tyler would have some. Ms. Morgan would throw up.

As soon as we got to school I looked carefully at Ms. Morgan. She didn't look allergic.
During free reading time, I wrote her a note.

Dear Ms. Morgan:
Are you alergick?
Your friend, Katie Jordan

During afternoon recess, she wrote me
back.
Dear Katie,
I am only allergic to poison oak.
Your friend, Ms. Morgan

Before the end of school, I wrote back to her.

Dear Ms. Morgan,
We will not have any poison oak for
Thanksgiving Dinner.
Your friend, Katie Jordan

That night we ate an early supper. Dad
made hot dogs. "Tonight, we practice good
manners," he told Tyler.

The meal went fine until suddenly Tyler
spit everything out of his mouth onto his plate.
"Look," he said, poking at the mess with his

finger, "mustard and ketchup and hot dog is pretty!"

Dad frowned. "No," he said. "NOT pretty." He took Tyler's plate to the kitchen. "You're finished, young man."

"Claire's turkey monster will know about this," I whispered.

Tyler's face turned white. He got down from the table and went to play with his trucks. He wasn't singing any songs. The house was strangely quiet.

"All right," Dad said as soon as the dishes were cleared away. "This recipe had better be easy."

"It's for the time-stressed woman," I said, opening the magazine.

"What about the time-stressed man?"

"You, too," I said.

We dumped canned sweet potatoes into a bowl. "Mash the potatoes," I read.

"Recipes don't tell you everything," Dad said. "These need to be drained." He tilted the potatoes over the sink until the juices were gone.

"Good thing you're helping me," I said.

"At least, they're cooked." Dad started to mash. "Already soft."

"I need help," Tyler called from the living room. "I need help."

Dad put down the masher. "Back in a minute," he said.

I measured a half-teaspoon of cinnamon and a half-teaspoon of cloves and sprinkled them over the potatoes. I was good with measuring spoons. Dad had taught me how to make cookies.

"His cement truck got stuck under the recliner," Dad said when he came back. He beat the potatoes until all the lumps were gone. "These are going to be good," he said, licking the masher.

We spread the potatoes in a pan. I melted butter in the microwave, and we poured brown sugar mixed with the butter over the top. Dad turned on the broiler.

"This is the tricky part," he said. "The recipe says, 'Watch carefully to avoid over-browning.'"

"Over-browning? What do they mean?"

"BURNING." He slid the dish under the hot broiler and peered in. Before he could say more, the phone rang. "Mr. Flagstaff," Dad said. "Hello, sir. What did you think of the first section?"

A loud voice came through the phone.

Dad smiled. "Glad you like it."

"I need help," Tyler hollered. This time he was in the bathroom.

"A new section?" Dad reached for paper and pencil. I ran down the hall.

Tyler had wrapped the whole roll of toilet paper around himself. "I started with a little bit," he said.

"You look like an Egyptian mummy," I said. "Let's show Dad." I led him down the hallway since he couldn't even see.

In the family room, Dad bent over the table with the phone jammed against his ear. He wrote furiously. "Yes, sir," he said. "Yes, sir."

Just then, I heard sputtering and crackling from the kitchen. A thick cloud of smoke rolled out of the oven.

# 14
# Dad Makes a Deal

The new batteries in our smoke alarm worked fine.

"Hold on, Mr. Flagstaff," Dad yelled. He put down the phone and pulled open the oven door. Flames shot out. More smoke.

I grabbed our new fire extinguisher and thrust it toward him.

Dad wrestled it out of the box. He aimed and pulled the trigger.

Whoosh!

The flames disappeared. A horrible smell came out of the oven.

I threw open the back door and flicked on the fan.

Dad flapped a towel at the alarm until it finally stopped screeching.

All that time, Tyler had been clinging to Dad's leg like a sticky burr. Dad picked him up in his arms. He picked up the phone. "All under control, sir." The receiver buzzed against his ear.

"Just a little cooking project," Dad said. "I'll get right to work on that extra section you want." He hung up the phone. The three of us stared at each other. Tyler snuffled.

"His clients are coming for the report on Thursday morning," he said.

"But that's Thanksgiving."

"His clients are from Japan. They don't celebrate Thanksgiving." He leaned toward me. "Katie," he said, and I knew what he would say before he even began. "About Ms. Morgan coming for dinner . . ."

Tears burned my eyes. I turned away from him so he wouldn't see them. "I want a real Thanksgiving," I blubbered.

"I don't understand," he said, "why this is so important."

"I want us to do what real. . ." I started, and then, I couldn't even finish.

"What real families do?"

I nodded.

"Katie," he said, "don't you see that we *are* a real family? That we don't have to do anything different?"

"We don't do things the way . . ." I couldn't finish again.

"The way Claire and Mr. Plummer do them?"

I nodded. A tear rolled down my cheek. I brushed it away.

Dad rubbed Tyler's back with long, slow rubs. "That's them, honey. They aren't any more real than we are."

"We'll get more canned sweet potatoes," I said, blinking back my tears. "We'll skip the over-browning part. You said they were delicious before we burned them. Remember?"

Tyler buried his face in Dad's shoulder. "I don't want any Thanksgiving."

"I'll call Ms. Morgan," Dad said. "I'll tell her the truth. That I have a work emergency.

Remember? Mr. Flagstaff wants that report Wednesday night."

My throat filled up with lumps. I couldn't answer.

Dad looked at Tyler. "What's this all over you?" he asked. "You look like an Egyptian mummy." He lifted some toilet paper and peeked under. "Is there a mummy under here?"

Tyler pulled his thumb out of his mouth. He snuffled. Then, he giggled. Pretty soon, he and Dad were rolling around on the floor just as if things were still fine.

While Dad put Tyler to bed, I put on my cranberry-popcorn necklace. I switched on the porch light and looked at the beautiful festoons. I went back in and studied the lists on my bulletin board.

Why was Dad so worried about cooking a turkey? He loved making pizzas. Could turkeys be that much harder? I reached for *Beautiful Living* and turned to page 39. A half-hour later, I went to tell Dad goodnight.

"I've got great news," I told him. "I read all about it. I can do the turkey by myself.

All I have to do is wash it and dry it and stick it in the oven for five hours. It's easy."

"I tried to phone Ms. Morgan," Dad said, "but her line was busy." His hand moved toward the phone on his desk.

"Think how much I'll learn," I told him. "This is good for my character."

He picked up the phone. Set it back down. "Your character could use some work."

"Tyler's character, too," I said. "He might stop playing with his food."

"The two of you used to be friends," Dad said. "Now, you squabble all the time."

"He's just scared of the Plummers' turkey."

"And who got him scared?"

I looked away.

Dad finally took his hand off the phone. He got a stern look on his face. "Okay. I have one rule. If you do this, you have to do it *with* Tyler."

"With Tyler!"

"He can help you decorate."

"He doesn't know how."

"You have to make it as much fun for him as

it is for you." Dad rubbed his forehead. "I can't believe I'm saying yes to this. It's insane."

All at once, I realized he'd said "yes."

"It'll be so easy," I said. "You'll see." I gave him a big goodnight hug and ran to my room before he could change his mind.

# 15
# Tower of Trouble

On Tuesday, Claire told the whole class about her Thanksgiving plans. "My father says it will be a wonderful dinner," she said. "Just like when my mother did it."

Ms. Morgan gave Claire a hug. "You miss your mom, don't you," she said in a soft voice. All at once, Claire's eyes were red and her face got puffy. It stayed puffy until Ms. Morgan chose her to take the attendance list to the office.

After school, Dad came into the kitchen when I was getting a snack. "Remember," he said. "If you're going to work on Thanksgiving stuff, I want Tyler to be part of it."

"I have to cook."

Dad blew out a worried breath.

"It'll be fine," I told him. "He can stir."

Tyler pushed a chair up to the counter and climbed up.

"We're making Green Beans Deluxe, Tyler." I opened the cans and handed him a wooden spoon. "There's a recipe, and we have to do everything right."

Tyler loved stirring. Green beans flipped across the counter and stuck to the wall. They spilled on the floor. They crawled up his shirt. They looked like green worms.

"Enough stirring," I said. When I poured what was left into a baking dish, the dish was only half-full. "There's not enough," I said.

Tyler beat the wooden spoon on the counter and mushroom soup splattered into the toaster. "Put popcorn in," he said.

I ate a green bean, and then I ate a piece of popcorn. They went together fine. With popcorn mixed in, the green beans filled up the dish.

"A good idea, huh," Tyler said. "About the popcorn."

"We wouldn't have needed it," I answered, "if you hadn't spilled."

"You're crabby," Tyler said. He went off to play with his trucks while I strung festoons as fast as I could. So much to do.

"I can make the Cranberry Tower tonight," I told Dad after dinner. "But I have to borrow a dish from Claire."

"Ask nicely," he said.

At Claire's house everything sparkled. Her dining room table was already set with a white cloth and real goblets. Blue and white china. Real napkins. A golden centerpiece of gourds.

"It's so pretty," Claire said with a sigh.

Mr. Plummer came into the room rolling up his shirt sleeves. "Tonight we wrap chocolate truffles in foil," he said. "We're having a truffle treasure hunt just before Thanksgiving dinner." He glanced at his watch and went into the kitchen.

When I went back home, I noticed all the porches on my street. Almost every one had decorations. All the real families were celebrating. Would I get it together? Would our

Thanksgiving be good enough for Ms. Morgan?

As soon as I opened our front door, I saw big trouble. Trucks and building blocks, Legos, and Tinker Toys. Our dining room table bristled with old food and Tyler's newspapers. I saw popcorn and cranberries and Egyptian mummy toilet paper. In the kitchen, green worms crawled across the vinyl.

Too much! Too much to do!

The Cranberry Tower took forever. I wanted it to be better than the magazine one, so at the last minute I dumped in good things like chocolate chips, little marshmallows, and raisins. When I finished, I showed Dad the refrigerator. Every shelf held bowls of red stuff. "It'll be thick in the morning," I told him, "Then I get to stack it all up."

"Time for bed," he said. He was looking at the green worms on the floor.

First thing Wednesday morning, I ran to check the bowls. I touched one with my finger. My finger went right in. "Soupy," I yelled. "It's still soupy."

"My head hurts," Tyler said. "I think that

turkey came over and bit me."

Dad fed every other bite of his cereal to Tyler. "Don't get sick, my boy. This is the last day for my report." He leaned his cheek against Tyler's cheek and closed his eyes. Testing for fever.

"Something else to worry about," I said. "We'll never be ready for tomorrow." I went to check the red stuff in the refrigerator. My finger went right in again.

I was too worried to eat. I dumped my cereal into the garbage. I brushed my teeth and put on my jacket. Acting like a real family was impossible for us.

It was time to face the facts.

It was time to uninvite Ms. Morgan.

# 16
# Who Is Coming to Dinner?

All day, I watched for a chance to talk to Ms. Morgan. At morning recess, she helped Ben with his science project. At afternoon recess, she met with some other teachers. Finally, it was time to go home, and I still hadn't uninvited her. I went to stand by her desk as the other kids left.

"Ms. Morgan," I said. "Something very bad—"

"Katie," she said with a big smile. "I want to tell you how excited I am." She stacked our spelling papers together and pushed them into her briefcase. "Holidays are hard when you're all alone," she said, taking her green and pink jacket off the hook and putting it on. "Here I am in Oregon, and my whole family is back in Minnesota." She bent down to look into my eyes. "I'm so happy you invited me."

I smiled back at Ms. Morgan. I wanted to tell her everything. But how could I? I couldn't make her be all alone on Thanksgiving. "See you tomorrow," I said. I ran outside to find Dad and Tyler.

All the way home, Tyler was a singing recycle collection truck. "Clang, clang, clankity clank," he yelled. "Roar, bam bam boom. Ding, ding, ding. The ding part is for when I back up," he told us.

"He doesn't have a fever," I said.

"He's fine. He spent most of the day at day care." Dad speeded up and, of course, Tyler's song got louder.

"Did the Cranberry Tower get stiff?" I had to run to keep up.

"Not yet," Dad said. "It's delicious though."

"You weren't supposed to eat any."

"You made plenty. I think we should call it Cranberry Swamp. Or maybe Cranberry Lakes."

"That's not funny," I told him.

After a quick dinner, we ran around getting ready for Mr. Flagstaff, picking up trucks and toys from the hallway.

At seven o'clock, the doorbell rang. I opened the door.

Mr. Flagstaff was very tall. "Hello, young lady," he said. He snapped his big black umbrella closed and stood it against the porch wall.

Dad came into the hallway with the stack of reports in his arms. "I think you'll like it, sir," he said.

"I'm sure I will," Mr. Flagstaff said. He turned and looked into the living room. Tyler had started a new bridge there with his big Legos. "My wife took that toy to my grandson," he said. "Stanley is three. He and I were going to play with those this weekend. Here I am, stuck in tomorrow's meeting. Not much of a Thanksgiving for me."

"Too bad," Dad said.

"Meeting starts at eight A.M. It'll last quite a few hours. No way I can get to Boise to be with my family. I'll be alone."

"Mr. Flagstaff," I said. I swallowed hard. "Would you like," I swallowed again, "to come to our house for Thanksgiving dinner?"

Dad's face looked like he was counting up glasses and napkins again. "That meeting might go all day, don't you think?"

"Not at all," Mr. Flagstaff said. "They fly back to Japan in the afternoon. Perhaps I could come. Perhaps I could."

Mr. Flagstaff handed Dad the reports and went into the living room. "The end of this bridge needs better support, young man. Engineers know these things. We need a thick book."

Mr. Flagstaff slid a dictionary under the Legos while Tyler held the bridge for him. "We can make these bridges even better tomorrow," Mr. Flagstaff said.

"All right!" Tyler yelled.

As soon as Mr. Flagstaff left, Dad turned to me. "I want the whole truth. WHO ELSE IS COMING TO DINNER?"

"All the others couldn't come," I said. "This is good, Dad. Mr. Flagstaff and Ms. Morgan can talk to each other when we're too busy."

He rubbed his eyes and shook his head. Then, he went to get his lists.

Later that night, Dad bought a huge turkey and more groceries. Even later than that, I went to bed. For the first time in ages, I went to sleep happy.

Tyler wasn't sick. Dad's report was done. We had our turkey. Now, everything would be fine.

# 17
# Harder Than a Rock

The next morning, I woke up early and ran to the kitchen. Dad was there looking at the turkey. He tapped it with his finger. "It's still frozen. Hard frozen. I don't know much about turkeys," he said. "But I think you aren't supposed to cook them until they thaw. And I think thawing takes a long time."

"Oh no!" I wailed. "The turkey is the most important thing!"

Dad picked up the phone. "We need a turkey expert."

A few minutes later, Claire and Mr. Plummer and Dad and I crowded around the turkey. We stared at it in silence.

"Expecting a crowd?" Mr. Plummer asked.

"It was the only one left at the store," Dad said.

Mr. Plummer knocked on the turkey. It spun round and round on the counter.

"Wow," Claire said. "Harder than a rock."

When the turkey stopped spinning, Mr. Plummer peered at its wrapper. "It says it takes three to four hours to thaw if you put it in cold water." He glanced at the sink. It was full of dishes.

"The bathtub," Dad said.

Mr. Plummer consulted his watch. "What time is your dinner?"

Dad looked at his watch too. "Our company comes at three. We eat at four," he said.

I stared at him in surprise. He sounded as organized as Mr. Plummer.

"Three to four hours in the tub. Five to six hours in the oven. It's now seven A.M." Mr. Plummer rubbed his chin. "That's close. Very close."

"We'll try it," Dad said.

"Hard to do these holidays right," Mr. Plummer said.

At the door, Claire turned back to me. "I'm a little worried," she said, "about these ivy things on your porch."

I looked at my festoons. "I like them."

"They look like poison oak," she said.

I slammed the door. Poison oak—the one thing Ms. Morgan was allergic to. I hated Thanksgiving!

In the bathtub, the turkey bobbed like a big white ship. We threw wet towels over it till it stayed under water. "Three hours," Dad said, looking at his watch. "Wish we had more time."

Tyler woke up. "Today is Thanksgiving Day," I told him. "We're going to have company. You have to be really good at the table."

He wasn't listening. He ran into the living room and peeked out the window. "The turkey monster is still dead," he said. "When it gets alive, you know what?"

"What?"

"I'm going to tame it!" He shivered and jumped up and down. "Turkeys are really scary, Katie."

I laughed. "You're really silly."

His face got serious. "Will you come with me, Katie? You could maybe hold my hand?"

"No way," I told him. "If you're going to be that silly, you can do it all by yourself."

"You used to be nice," Tyler said. "Now you're mean."

"That's not true," I said.

After a quick breakfast, Dad and I cleaned the house. By nine o'clock, green worms no longer crawled across the kitchen floor. The dishwasher had been run. Except for Tyler's bridges in the living room, the house looked pretty good.

We couldn't find a tablecloth. Instead, we put a white sheet over the table, and it hung down to the floor. Tyler crawled underneath. While he couldn't see me, I set my smiling turkey on the table.

"Come in here," Tyler said, poking his head out. "It's a hidey hole."

I rushed to get the duster. "We're too busy," I said.

"No, we're not," Dad said. He crawled under the sheet and then poked his head out again.

"We have time for one story in the hidey hole. Come join us."

"No," I shouted. "We don't have time!"

The phone rang. I ran to answer it. It was Claire.

"Is it thawed yet?" she asked.

"Not yet," I said.

"I hope your company doesn't get poison oak," she said.

"I'll keep her away from it," I said.

"Keep WHO away?"

I hung up. While I opened cans of sweet potatoes, Dad and Tyler finished their story. Then, Dad went to clean the bathroom, except for the tub. That was when Tyler noticed the centerpiece.

"Turkeys scare me," he hollered. He pulled on the sheet. The turkey poster glided toward him.

"Stop it, Tyler!" I ran across the room. Before I could reach him, he ripped my turkey into shreds. I grabbed Tyler's arm and shook him. He burst into tears. Dad came running.

"This was my favorite turkey!" I shouted.

I stomped around the room, waving turkey pieces in the air. "I hate you, Tyler. Now, our table is ugly." I hurled the turkey pieces onto the floor and fled down the hall to my room.

A few minutes later, Dad and Tyler crept in. Tyler patted my shoulder. "I'm sorry, Katie," he whispered. I sat up and glared at him.

"Tyler thought up a new centerpiece," Dad said.

I dragged down the hall and looked at the table. They'd put Tyler's dump truck on the table. They'd filled it with cranberries and popcorn. The green truck, the red berries and the white popcorn were pretty.

Tyler and Dad grinned at me.

"It's not the same," I said. "But thanks."

I went back to making the sweet potatoes. After I dumped them into a big bowl, Dad mashed them fast. "This is what practice can do," he said. "We are terrific cooks."

I tried to swallow over the lump in my throat. "But we have way too many things to worry about," I said. "Now I wish nobody was coming."

He nodded. "Next year . . ." he said.

"Let's wear pajamas and watch the game on TV," I said.

"Sounds like heaven." He handed me a package of orange paper napkins. "These go next to the forks."

At eleven-thirty, Tyler ate his lunch under the table. Then, Dad tucked him in for his nap.

"Soon as I wake up," Tyler told us, "I'm going to do it."

"Do what?" Dad asked.

Tyler pointed across the street and shivered. "Tame him!"

# 18
# Big Trouble

Once Tyler was in bed, Dad and I followed the directions on the turkey wrapper and stuck the huge, cold thing into the oven. "Cross your fingers that it cooks in time," Dad said.

Then we set out plates and glasses.

"Go easy on Tyler," Dad said. "He's only three, you know."

I suddenly remembered saying the same thing to Claire a couple of weeks ago. Had I gotten like her? Always pointing out the bad things? "I'm afraid Ms. Morgan will throw up when she sees him eat," I said.

"She won't throw up," Dad said. "He's a pretty cute kid."

"He's being brave about that turkey in the Plummers' yard," I said. "He says he's going to tame it."

"I wonder what he means." Dad yawned. "I'm going to shower and take a nap." He disappeared into his bedroom.

I made the appetizers while Dad's shower ran. Every few minutes I flicked on the oven light. The turkey still looked stiff. As I put the appetizers on a plate, I hoped they were pretty enough. But I hardly cared any more. I shoved them into the refrigerator and went to stare at the turkey. It was browning a little.

At two-thirty, Dad came into the kitchen to check the turkey. "It won't be ready in time," he said as he tried to poke a fork into it. "We could tell them to come later, but there's no way to phone Mr. Flagstaff. He's in that meeting."

Trouble filled my chest and made me want to cry. "They'll be here in half an hour," I wailed.

Dad grabbed the phone book and flipped pages. "A restaurant," he muttered. Then, he tossed the phone book into the drawer.

"We'd never get a reservation now. There's got to be cooked turkey at the store." He jingled his car keys at me. "Get Tyler up and dressed. If our company comes, give them appetizers."

As he left, I put the plate of appetizers on the coffee table and ran to Tyler's room. "Tyler?" I said.

No answer.

I shoved all the stuffed animals onto the floor. The bed was empty. Tyler was gone.

# 19
# Where Did the Treasures Go?

Tyler was nowhere in the house. I grabbed my jacket and ran out the front door. Cars lined both sides of our street. Of course! Claire's company had come.

Had Tyler gone to tame the turkey? He knew better than to cross the street by himself. Didn't he?

I suddenly remembered how he liked to hold my hand when he was scared. "Tyler," I called. "I'm coming! I'll help you." Tears filled my eyes as I ran across the street. On Claire's front lawn, something glittered at me. I picked it up. A truffle. I stuck it in my pocket.

Just then, Claire's front door opened. About a hundred people came out. Mr. Plummer was with them. He blew a whistle and a strange gobble sound came out of it. "Treasure hunt time," he announced. "Gobble, gobble."

I hid behind the turkey.

"What a clever idea," a lady in a purple hat said. She came down the porch steps, looking into the gourds and squashes for treasures.

But this would take too long. I had to find Tyler. I stood up. "My little brother is lost," I said to the purple hat lady. "Please look for him while you look for the treasures."

Claire lifted her blue Pilgrim skirts and flounced down the steps. "You're not supposed to be here," she said.

"Tyler's out somewhere by himself." I swallowed a sob. "He needs me."

"I'm sure he's not here." Claire straightened her Pilgrim hat and tightened the blue bow under her chin. "We didn't invite him, remember?"

"Here's one," someone said.

"I give up," said a tall man.

"Look what I found." Purple Hat held out a blue bowl. "It's full of unpopped popcorn," she said, "It was in front of that wooden turkey."

I ran to her. "That's our bowl! Tyler *has* been here!"

Just then the Pilgrim lady on the porch swing began to move. All eyes turned to watch. "It's turkey food," a little voice said. "Put it back."

I ran onto the porch as Tyler crawled out from under the Pilgrim lady's wide skirts. I wrapped my arms around him. "Are you okay?"

"I brought him popcorn," Tyler whispered to me. "He's tame now. I know he's tame. He laid eggs for me."

"At least we found a lost child." Claire's dad held the door open for all his company. "Maybe the birds got some of the truffles. We hid a lot of them."

"Doesn't matter," the tall man said. "This is a great party. Thanks to you and Claire."

Claire fluffed her skirts and pranced up the porch steps as Tyler set our blue bowl of popcorn in front of the turkey.

"He didn't lay eggs," I told him. "He can't. He's not real."

Just then a car drove slowly down the street and pulled into our driveway. Ms. Morgan!

My stomach churned. My party was starting. I wasn't ready.

# 20
# Poison Oak!

**M**s. Morgan's here," I called to Tyler. "Come on!"

Claire spun around. "Who's here?" She grabbed her skirts and raced after us.

"Happy Thanksgiving!" Ms. Morgan said. She stepped out of her car and reached back in for a package.

"*Ms. Morgan* is your company?" Claire stared at me, an angry look on her face.

Ms. Morgan turned back to us, holding her pies. "Apple and pumpkin," she said. "Hello, Claire. I didn't realize you lived right across the street from Katie."

"You should be coming to MY house," Claire said. "Not to hers."

Ms. Morgan put her finger to her lips. Then she looked up and down the street. "Just look at your beautiful porches," she said. "You've turned your street into a Thanksgiving celebration."

Claire and I stopped glaring at each other.

"Thank you," we both said.

"We have a ton of people," Claire told Ms. Morgan. "One lady said our party should be in the newspaper."

"I believe it," Ms. Morgan answered. "I see you're wearing a Pilgrim costume, Claire. Very nice."

"I'm glad you like it," Claire lifted her skirts and turned slowly around.

My clothes! I looked down at my jeans and soggy tennis shoes. Nothing was turning out right. And why wasn't Dad back yet with the turkey?

As Claire ran back to her house, Tyler dragged Ms. Morgan and her pies onto our porch.

She looked back at me and smiled. "I love these vines," she said. She lifted her hand

and reached toward the green leaves.

"Don't . . . touch!" I said.

"I'll be very careful." Ms. Morgan  brushed her hand gently down along the leaves. "So pretty," she said.

And then she brushed her hand back up.

I couldn't speak. Ms. Morgan was a goner.

"Wash it off!" I finally gasped, but by then, Tyler had pulled her through the door, and she didn't hear me.

I started up the porch steps. Ms. Morgan was going to hate me. I would never, ever live this down.

I heard a car coming. Our car.

I ran back toward the driveway and watched Dad park behind Ms. Morgan's car. Now we'd have a turkey. Brown and beautiful like the ones in the magazines. The turkey would fix everything.

But Dad opened his door and held up his hands. They were empty.

# 21
# The Last Great Idea

Dad's face was pale. "Half the stores were closed. The others had no turkey. It's all sold out." He stepped out of the car and sagged against it. "What a disaster!"

"Hello," someone called. Mr. Flagstaff strode down the walk. He grabbed Dad's hand and pumped it up and down. "They said the report was well organized and very detailed." Mr. Flagstaff's gray eyebrows arched up in happy lines.

"Come on, Mr. Friend," Tyler shouted from the front door. "Come and play with us."

Mr. Flagstaff hurried toward the porch. "Okay if I go right in?"

"Watch out for . . ." I started to say, but Mr. Flagstaff had gone.

"Watch out for what?" Dad asked.

"Claire says the festoons are poison oak. Ms. Morgan touched them! She's going to get a rash!"

Dad strode up the steps and looked at the leaves. "This is ornamental ivy."

My eyes filled with tears of relief. "Are you sure?"

"I know ornamental ivy when I see it," Dad said. "No question about it."

"But Claire said—"

He glanced across the street and looked back at me. "Your decorations are fine. They look wonderful."

"Just a minute," someone called. We turned to see Claire and her dad coming out their front door. They raced across the street.

"Have to be quick," Mr. Plummer said, looking at his watch. "Our company is filling their plates. I imagine your turkey's still not cooked. No way it could be." He swallowed and looked again at his watch. "Claire thought you might bring Ms. Morgan to our house. And you'd come too, of course. Join us for dinner. Ahem. Tyler, too."

Claire wrinkled her nose. "We'll put down lots of newspapers."

"That's a nice invitation," Dad said. "But we have two guests. My employer, Mr. Flagstaff, is also here."

"I'm sure they'd rather be at our house," Claire said. "Everyone really likes it."

"Our house is okay, too," I said. It really was.

Dad looked down at me. "Except, we don't have a . . ." Then he stopped.

"I have a great idea," I said. I thought fast. My Cranberry Tower was a swamp. But it was delicious. My centerpiece was a truck. But it was pretty. Maybe, the main thing—the turkey—could change, too. I nodded at Claire and put my hand into Dad's. "We'll be fine," I said.

Dad looked at me and a little smile grew in his eyes. He turned to Mr. Plummer. "Katie's thought of something," he said.

As the Plummers went back home, Dad put

his arm around me. "Honey," he whispered, "What will we put on the big platter?"

"Pizza," I said. "Your famous pizza."

He yanked off his glasses and blinked his eyes. "I was hoping you'd say that!" He grabbed my hands and swung me up the porch steps.

## 22
## The Thanksgiving Platter

In the living room, Ms. Morgan, Mr. Flagstaff, and Tyler crept across the rug, piling more books under bridges. Trucks and buses waited in line to cross over them.

Tyler had filled his garbage truck with my appetizers. "Get your happy-tizers," he said. Something else was in the truck, too. Shiny foil-wrapped things. Truffles! Lots of them!

"Turkey eggs," Tyler said. "That turkey is sure my friend."

I added my truffle to the pile. "That's why nobody could find any."

Dad cleared his throat. "I have an announcement," he said. "The turkey isn't ready."

"We have something else to eat," I said. "But it's not made yet."

"Could I help?" Ms. Morgan asked. "It would feel just like home."

A few minutes later, we were all in the kitchen. Dad thawed bread dough in the microwave and took orders for pizza toppings. Soon the half-cooked turkey was out of the oven, and the pizza was in.

"We have lots more food too," Dad said. "Wait till you see Katie's Cranberry Tower."

"Ahem," I said. "It's really Cranberry Swamp."

"Or maybe Cranberry Lakes," Dad said. "It didn't gel, but it's delicious."

I pulled the vegetables out of the refrigerator and handed them to Mr. Flagstaff.

"Let me be in charge of heating these." Mr. Flagstaff carried them to the microwave. "My specialty," he said, "is pushing buttons."

"Get your happy-tizers," Tyler kept saying as he drove his garbage truck from person to person. Then, he sang us a garbage truck appetizer song.

"That's silly," I started to say. But just in time, I remembered I didn't want to sound like Claire. "Great song, Tyler," I said.

"That song was for you, Katie," Tyler said. "Because you came to save me from the monster."

Dad smiled at me.

We poured sparkling cider into glasses. At last, we had almost everything on the table.

Mr. Flagstaff hoisted Tyler into his chair.

Ms. Morgan held her camera ready.

Tyler munched on centerpiece popcorn.

Dad marched in like a French waiter, holding the big platter high in the air. "My famous pizza," he announced.

I held my breath. Goosebumps popped out on my arms. Thanksgiving dinner with no turkey? Was it really okay?

Mr. Flagstaff leaned forward and clapped his hands. "Bravo!" he said. He rubbed his belly and sighed with happiness.

"We're having a feast!" Ms. Morgan said. "I love pizza." She snapped a photo of Dad. Then she snapped me putting a big spoon into the Cranberry Swamp.

"I'm so thankful," she said as she sat back down, "to be with a real family today."

Dad and I looked at each other.

"That's us," I said.

Anne Warren Smith grew up in the Adirondack Mountains of upstate New York. She now lives in Corvallis, Oregon, where she has raised two daughters and several dogs. She teaches creative writing, kayaks the Oregon lakes and rivers, noodles on her guitar, and knits sweaters for her granddaughter. She is the author of two other novels for children and young adults, *Blue Denim Blues* and *Sister in the Shadow*.

Every Thanksgiving, for as long as she can remember, there's been a turkey on her table. But that could always change.